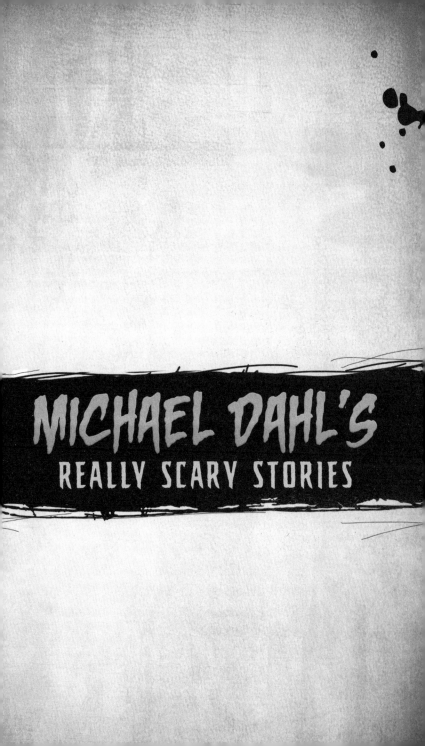

MICHAEL DAHL'S
REALLY SCARY STORIES

Michael Dahl's Really Scary Stories
are published by Stone Arch Books,
A Capstone Imprint
1710 Roe Crest Drive
North Mankato, Minnesota 56003
www.capstonepub.com

Library of Congress Cataloging-in-Publication Data
Dahl, Michael, author.
  The voice in the boys' room and other scary tales / by Michael
Dahl ; illustrated by Xavier Bonet.
       pages cm. -- (Michael Dahl's really scary stories)
  Summary: Logan is disturbed by a mysterious mumbling voice in the
boys' room, but when he finds a cell phone floating in the toilet, and
reaches in to retrieve it he is caught in a trap — and that is only
one of the chilling stories in this collection.
  ISBN 978-1-4965-0596-5 (library binding) -- ISBN 978-1-4965-2334-1
(ebook pdf)
1. Fear--Juvenile fiction. 2. Horror tales, American. [1. Horror
stories. 2. Short stories.] I. Bonet, Xavier, 1979- illustrator. II.
Title.
  PZ7.D15134Vo 2016
  813.54--dc23
  [Fic]

                                            2015001863

Designer: Hilary Wacholz
Image Credits: Dmitry Natashin

Printed in China by Nordica
0415/CA21500548
032015   008842NORDF15

THE VOICE IN THE BOYS' ROOM
AND OTHER SCARY TALES

By Michael Dahl

Illustrated by
Xavier Bonet

STONE ARCH BOOKS
a capstone imprint

TABLE OF CONTENTS

Dear Reader,

My friend Thom invited me to an unusual Halloween party.

Each guest had to bring a scary story to read. There were only seven of us. After dinner, Thom lit candles and then turned out the lights.

One by one, the guests told their tales.

Some stories were from comics, some from books. One guest had printed his out from the computer. My story was the true tale of a haunted coal mine. Each story gave us goose bumps.

You, too, have been invited to a party. By opening this book you have accepted the invitation. Don't worry if you didn't bring your own scary story. There are plenty here.

You don't need to turn out the lights, either.

THE GOOSE BUMPS WILL STILL COME.

Michael Dahl

DON'T MAKE A WISH

Nina stood up and faced her giant chocolate birthday cake.

"Make a wish! Make a wish!" her friends shouted. They crowded around the table to get a good look at the birthday girl.

Nina's mom and dad stood nearby, smiling, presents in their arms.

"Make a wish, honey," said her mom.

Nina thought hard. Wishes were serious. She bent toward the nine candles and blew.

"Yeah!" everyone shouted. The candles went out.

But a breeze kept blowing. A strong breeze. It blew across the table, fluttering napkins and shoving aside balloons. Party hats went flying. Birthday presents tumbled onto the floor. The wind whistled louder and louder.

Nina didn't move. She stood still, confetti and streamers swirling around her. "It's coming true," she said.

Nina's mom fought against the wind to reach her side. "What are you talking about?" she yelled. "What did you wish for?"

"I wished Great-Aunt Sally could come to my birthday party," Nina said.

"No, honey," said her mom. "Your Great-Aunt Sally died last week. Don't you remember?"

The doorbell rang.

"Someone's at the door!" yelled a kid.

Nina's parents frowned. Was it a late party guest?

Dad marched toward the door.

The wind grew stronger. It rushed against the huge birthday cake.

"No one's out here," Nina's dad called out.

Frosting slid down the sides of the cake. The candles flew into the air. The top of the cake exploded, pushed up from inside. Up rose a round white skull, dripping with chocolate. It turned to face Nina.

"Happy birthday, dear," said the skull. "I didn't think I'd make it."

HAIKUKU

The minute arrives.

Door opens — I run! I scream!

The clock pulls me back.

BLINK!

The eye doctor puts drops in my eyes.

"This won't hurt," he says. And he's right. It doesn't hurt at all. There's a funny stinging on my eyeballs, but that's all.

"This is a new medicine," he says. "It should clear up that infection really quickly."

He's talking about the weird eye infection I got at school. Lots of kids were getting it — even a few teachers. It makes green crud come out of your eyes, and everything looks fuzzy. So my mom took me to see our eye doctor, Dr. Glass, this morning. I know. Glass. Funny, right?

"Don't rub your eyes for at least an hour," says the doctor.

My mom is leading me out of the office when Dr. G. stops us. "Oh, one other thing, Kevin," he says to me. "There's a little side effect."

"Side effect?" I repeat.

"You might feel a little dizzy," Dr. Glass says as he carefully reads the label on the bottle of medicine he dropped into my eyes just a minute ago.

Didn't he check it out before? I wonder. And suddenly I'm not feeling great about my visit.

"It seems you'll have double vision," he says. "It should wear off in a few hours. Nothing to worry about."

"Double vision?" I ask. I'm about to say, *What does that mean?* But suddenly I'm staring at two doctors, each holding a bottle in their right hand. *Okay,* I think. *I know what it means.*

My mom leads me out of the doctor's office, down the hall, and into the elevator. I hate elevators, but Dr. Glass's office is on the twenty-third floor of the medical building downtown.

There's no way I'd be able to climb down twenty-three flights of stairs.

My eyes feel hot. I start to rub them, but then my mom says, "Remember what the doctor said. Don't rub your eyes."

"They itch," I reply.

"Try not to think about it," she says.

"I'm *not* thinking about it," I say. "And they still itch."

"Hush!" she says, glancing around the elevator car. She's looking at the two other passengers, embarrassed.

I close my eyes, but they start to sting. When I open them again, the elevator has two more passengers.

Weird. I don't remember the elevator stopping. I didn't hear the little ding it makes when it stops at a floor. I didn't hear the footsteps of people getting on.

My eyes are hot, so I blink again. Now I see eight people in the elevator. *Oh yeah, double vision,* I remind myself. *My eyes are playing tricks.*

But the people in the elevator are acting oddly. I hear a woman gasp. A man says, "Let me off! Now!"

Blink.

Now the elevator is almost full. And what's even weirder, there are lots of people wearing the same clothes. Like they're clones or something. At first I thought it was just my eyes acting funny because of the drops. But people are starting to cram in tighter and tighter, so maybe there really are more people on the elevator.

Blink.

Without warning, I'm shoved up against the wall.

"Where are all these people coming from?" cries my mother.

And I realize I'm not only *seeing* doubles. There *are* doubles. Doubles of doubles. The number of passengers is doubling, and then doubling again. Each time I blink, more people pop into view. It isn't my eyes. It's really happening.

This is the most amazing thing that has ever happened to me. I can't help myself. I have to look again.

Blink.

Not a good idea.

I get pushed into a corner of the elevator. The air is stuffy, and someone just farted. Great.

"Push the stop button!" someone yells.

"Move your elbow!" says another.

"I can't reach the buttons," says a third. "It's too crowded."

How many people are there? How many bodies can the elevator hold? At least it feels like the elevator is still going down.

Thud.

The elevator stops. We're stuck between floors!

"Kevin!" I hear my mom's voice.

"I'm back here," I reply. I don't dare to look at her. I keep my eyes squeezed shut.

Four men near the front of the elevator all say at the same time, "We're on the main floor. This is the lobby. But the doors won't open."

Four women say, "Push the Open button."

Four more women say, "Can whoever is farting please stop?"

Eight men say, "It wasn't me!"

It's getting harder to breathe. We're running out of air. I can feel bodies squirming around me. I can hear people crying, shouting, moaning, giggling. (Some people are ticklish, I guess.)

"Kevin!" My mom's voice is getting weaker.

"I'm going to faint," a man next to me says.

Somewhere a woman whispers, "What we need is more force to open those doors."

Force! I think. More and more power pushing against the doors. This gives me an idea. It might be foolish, but I figure we can't stay in the elevator much longer. We need to get out one way or another.

I open my eyes.

I look at as many people as I can. Then I blink. And I keep on blinking.

More and more bodies fill the elevator. Bodies on top of bodies. Screaming bodies. Squirming bodies. The ceiling light is covered up, then it gets smashed in the squeeze. My knees are giving out from all the extra people weighing me down. The air is being sucked up faster and faster by the extra pairs of lungs.

A long, drawn-out groan shakes the elevator. And then — *bang!* — the crush of people burst the elevator doors apart. It worked! We spill out into the lobby like candy from a gumball machine.

My mom finds me after a few minutes. She hugs me and then grabs my arm and walks me outside.

"My eyes hurt!" I say. "I can't open them."

"That's fine, sweetie," she says.

She gets us onto a bus and back home safely, guiding me the whole way.

Alone in my room, I feel my way over to the bed. I figure I'll lie down, pull the covers over my head, and rest. Dr. Glass said the double vision would last a few hours. If I go to sleep now, when I wake up in the morning everything should be back to normal.

My feet hit something as I walk across the floor, and I stumble. My eyes fly open. Oh no!

I was looking at my bed when I fell. It didn't double. It looks a little fuzzy around the edges, but otherwise it has stayed the same.

That was lucky, I think. I sit on the edge of the bed and stare across the room at my dresser. The dresser with the mirror.

Blink.

Big mistake.

Too bad there aren't two beds in my room. I could use them now.

I mean, *we* could.

SNOW MONSTER

The sun was low in the sky. The clouds were so orange, they looked like they were on fire. There was a light breeze. The snow had stopped falling. It was perfect hunting weather.

Deer come out right before the sun sets. And there are a lot of deer where we live, just outside a small town in northern Wisconsin. North of our home there's a line of evergreens, which is the border of a large forest. Lots of deer trails lead into the trees. We were following one that morning.

I love being out in the woods with my father. When I was really young, he taught me how to recognize an animal's footprints.

In the woods that morning I could see the tracks of rabbits, fox, field mice, and, of course, deer.

It was cold enough to see our breath, but not too cold. Carefully and quietly we headed deep into the woods. We came to a small clearing. My father stopped suddenly.

He was looking down at the snow. "We'd better go back, son," he said.

"What is it?" I asked.

He shook his head and turned away, but I had to see. I ran over and looked at the snow. There were footprints I had never seen before. They were huge — at least four times bigger than my father's.

I looked at him. *The Geeshee Moogomon?* I wondered.

I had heard the stories. The Geeshee was a big, bloodthirsty beast that could change its shape and color. You never saw it until it was too late. It was a story adults told us to keep us from going into the deep woods. To keep us out of trouble. I'd never believed it was real.

My father was firm. "We're going home," he said. "Now."

Suddenly, I saw what else my father had seen. The dead body. A deer had fallen onto the snow. Blood spread out from it, red staining the white ground.

A scream pierced the air. A nearby tree seemed to explode. Bark flew off and hit my head.

"Hurry!" cried my father.

We both turned and took off across the snow, our tails flying behind us. I never looked back.

After several minutes, my father stopped. He lifted his head and howled. We had to warn our cousins and neighbors of the danger.

We took the long way home. "So the Geeshee won't be able to find us," my father said.

When we were finally inside our den, I raced to my mother. I snuggled as close as I could, hearing her heart beat beneath her beautiful fur.

For now, I was safe from the monster.

A PERFECT FIT

Fitting in. That's the hardest part about going to a new school, Lola thought.

New hallways, new teachers, new locker — all of it was hard at first. But fitting in and finding new friends was the worst.

And the worst part of fitting in, Lola thought, *is figuring out where to sit for lunch.* It was the biggest decision of her first day. Lola couldn't afford to make a mistake.

Standing near the wall of the cafeteria, Lola held her lunch tray and looked around. She was too new to have made any friends. No one expected her to sit with them. Lola was afraid to sit just anywhere. What if she sat at the wrong table? With the wrong kids, kids who also didn't fit in? For the rest of her middle school life, she would be known as a loser.

"Hey! Hey you!" Lola saw a girl in a bright-yellow sweater waving at her. She slowly walked over to the girl's table.

"You mean *me*?" asked Lola.

"Sit down," said the girl in the yellow sweater. "I'm Jordan." Then she introduced the other four girls at the table: Eva, Anna, Lillian, and Kate.

"And what is your name?" asked Jordan.

"Lola," she said, shyly.

"Lola? That's different," said Anna.

The girl named Lillian giggled.

"It's Spanish," said Eva. "Or Mexican."

"Oh. Are you, like, Mexican?" asked Kate.

Eva rolled her eyes.

"No," said Lola. "My mom just liked the name."

Jordan nodded. "It's very Hollywood," she said.

Lunchtime passed quickly. The girls talked about classes and teachers and what they had done over summer vacation. The cafeteria bell rang. Lola looked up at the caged clock. Lunch period was over? She was having so much fun that she hadn't noticed the time.

"Time to go, girls," said a teacher as she walked by.

When they got up from the table, Lola noticed something for the first time. Something odd. Each girl wore the same backpack. The backpacks were purple with white trim. Some of the girls had decorated theirs with stickers and key chains and buttons, but it was the same backpack.

As she gathered her own bag, Lola realized that all the girls had worn them while they ate. None of them had taken their backpacks off.

Maybe they're a club, thought Lola. *And that's, like, their uniform or something.*

"See ya," said Lola, with a little wave.

"Bye!" they all replied brightly. The five girls turned and walked away from the table. Five purple backpacks disappeared into the crowd of students.

For the next week, Lola always sat at the same table. She sometimes saw her lunch pals in the halls. She had classes with a few of them. Jordan (the girl who had waved at her), Anna, Eva, Lillian, and Kate. No matter where she saw them, they always wore their backpacks. Even while sitting in class.

What about PE class? Lola wondered. *They'd have to put them in their lockers then, right?*

One day, Lola heard two other girls in the hall talking about her friends.

"Those backpack girls are so fake," said one.

"They act all sweet," agreed the other one. "But then they say things behind your back."

Lola didn't think her new friends were fake. They had gone out of their way to be nice to her, to make her feel welcome. And they didn't gossip any more than everyone else did. Those girls in the hall were just jealous.

During Friday's lunch, when all the girls were seated, Anna leaned into the table and whispered, "Tomorrow night — sleepover!"

"Cool!"

"Yeah!"

"Fun!" the girls whispered back.

Jordan turned to Lola and said, "You're coming, right?"

"Oh, uh —" said Lola.

"Of course she's coming," said Anna.

Lola couldn't believe her luck. The first week of school was over, and she already had a group of cool friends. And now a sleepover party. Lola and her mother went to the mall that night and bought a new sleeping bag. Lola insisted on a backpack, too. She picked out a purple one. It wasn't the same brand the other girls had, but it was the right size. Lola liked the way it felt on her shoulders. She was sure it would help her fit in.

On Saturday night, Lola's dad drove her to Anna's house. "Have fun, honey!" he yelled to her as she ran toward the front door.

The other girls were already there. The party was filled with loud music, laughter, pizza, ice cream, and gossip. The entire night, even as the girls laid out their sleeping bags in the big family room at the back of the house, Jordan and her friends never took off their backpacks. Lola tried keeping hers on, but after a while it became uncomfortable.

In fact, Jordan came up to her during a break in the fun and helped Lola slip it off her shoulders. "It's not the same kind," she said to Lola.

Lola felt like someone had hit her in the stomach. *Those two girls in the hall were right,* she thought, her eyes filling with tears.

"What's wrong?" Kate asked, walking over to them.

These girls don't really like me, thought Lola. *I need to go. I'll just call Dad to come pick me up.*

"Her backpack," Jordan told Kate.

"Is that all?" Kate took Lola's hand. "Don't worry about it," she said. "We can help you find another one. Jordan's the queen of bargain stores, and I'm the queen of key chains!"

Jordan smiled at Lola. "You look good in purple, too," she said.

Lola wiped her eyes and smiled back. "Thanks," she said.

It was nearing midnight and all the girls were dressed for sleep, sitting or lying on their sleeping bags. The purple backpacks were still on their shoulders. Lola felt better. They were all talking and laughing when Anna's mother yelled down the hallway, "Lights out, girls!"

Anna rolled her eyes. "You heard her," she whispered. "Lights out, girls." The rest of them giggled.

With the lights off, the family room was surprisingly dark. As Lola snuggled into her sleeping bag, she heard rustling all around her. The girls were taking off their backpacks. *Finally*, thought Lola. Then it was quiet.

Lola woke up an hour later, needing to use the bathroom. Too much soda. She slipped out of her sleeping bag as quietly as she could and stood up in the dark. The other girls were sleeping. Someone was snoring. Someone else was mumbling in her sleep.

Lola remembered where the bathroom was and walked down the short hallway. On her way back, she snapped off the bathroom light and then stood still. Her eyes needed a few moments adjusting from the bright bathroom to the dark hallway. She didn't want to trip or fall over anyone.

Where was her sleeping bag? She stepped carefully, as if she were walking on the balance beam in gym class. Her foot hit someone's back.

"Oops. Sorry," she said.

Lola's eyes were growing more used to the dark. She could see the five shapes of the sleeping girls. She saw her empty sleeping bag. She looked down at the girl she had bumped into. It was Jordan.

Lola bent down. "Sorry," she whispered again. But Jordan didn't move.

Something about the position of her arms bothered Lola. She didn't know why, but she reached out to the sleeping girl and gently touched her arm.

It was cold. Not freezing cold, but it certainly wasn't giving off any warmth. It felt like plastic.

Lola heard the mumbling again. It came from beyond the circle of sleeping bags.

She spotted a shadow next to the wall. A pile of dark purple. *The backpacks,* Lola thought. That's where the girls had put them. But who was mumbling in her sleep?

Lola watched in terror as one of the backpacks moved. It swayed back and forth. It waddled across the carpet like a penguin. The shoulder straps hung on either side like skinny arms. A thin white line appeared on the front of the backpack. A fold in the purple fabric. A fold that seemed to turn into a smile.

"Don't worry," whispered the backpack. "We'll find one for you, Lola." It was Jordan's voice.

Lola was about to scream when she felt something soft and bumpy brush against her leg. She glanced down and saw more backpacks. The one nearest her leg opened its mouth and Lola could see rows and rows of tiny, sharp teeth.

"We'll help you find a new one. The right one," said the backpack.

The backpack's voice was Lola's voice.

Lola fell onto her sleeping bag. The purple creature shuffled toward her and patted her back. "Yes, yes. A new backpack," it said gently. "She will be a perfect fit."

SIDEWALKS
FROM
OUTER
SPACE

What a movie! I mean, what a *movie*!

We burst out of the theater — my friend Carlos and I, and my big brother, Caleb, and his buddy Ethan. We couldn't stop talking about it.

"Awesome, dude!" Carlos said.

"Totally awesome," I said.

Stealth Invasion IV: Alien Destruction. Best. Movie. Ever. The absolute best in the series.

"I want to see it again," said Caleb.

"We are so seeing it again," said Carlos.

"I can't," said Ethan. "Gotta get home. It's late."

It was late. After midnight. The moon and stars were shining. My mom and Carlos's parents had let us stay out late because we were with Caleb and Ethan, who were sixteen.

We walked down the sidewalk, past a corner where people were getting on a city bus. Its doors hissed shut as it pulled away from the curb. The greenish lights inside the bus and the tinted windows made the passengers inside look like aliens. Visitors to our planet were taking off in their silver ship. *Swoosh!*

"The alien destructor suits were cool!" I said.

"Their blue starships were even cooler," said Carlos.

Caleb snorted. "Which is why the whole thing would never work," he said. "Not in real life. Not in a million years."

"Yeah," said Ethan.

I stopped walking. "What do you mean?" I said.

"Alien invasion," said Caleb. "If their ships were coming at us like that, in the open, we would have seen the ⸻rom miles away."

"The armies of Earth would have banded together," said Ethan. "By the time they reached the planet, we'd be ready for them."

"We sure wouldn't be surprised, like the army dudes in the movie," said Caleb. "The movie's called *Stealth Invasion*. Where was the stealth part?"

"Good one, dude," agreed Ethan.

We started walking again. We were ten blocks from our house. Carlos was sleeping over with us, but Ethan lived a little farther away. The four of us were the only ones on the sidewalk. I could feel warmth rising from the cement, even though the night was cool. Cool and dark. And each block got darker than the last. Why weren't the streetlights working?

Ethan was chuckling to himself. I guess he was still thinking about Caleb's remark that the aliens weren't stealthy. Caleb sort of had a point.

"If you're so smart, how would you do it?" asked Carlos.

"Yeah, how would you do it?" I said.

Caleb usually waves his arms around when he talks big. This time he didn't. He stopped in the middle of the block, where the shadows were thickest. He leaned in close to us, like he didn't want anyone else to hear. "Like the movie says, boys — stealth," Caleb said. "Hidden. Secret. Camouflaged."

"I know what stealth means," I said.

"If I were an alien, I'd already be here," said Caleb. "I would have been here for years by now. Dozens of years. Hiding. Just waiting for the right time. Then I'd attack and catch everyone by surprise. That's how an invasion works."

"Good one, dude," said Ethan.

"Where would you hide?" Carlos asked quietly.

Caleb looked around. He stared down at his shoes. He snorted again. "We don't know what aliens really look like, right?" he said. "So why couldn't they be disguised as something normal you see everyday?"

"Something normal?" said Ethan seriously.

Caleb nodded. "Like . . . a sidewalk."

Carlos laughed. Ethan didn't smile.

A sidewalk, I thought. *Why not?*

"One night," said Caleb, "when we were all asleep, the aliens came. The aliens were long like giant snakes. Their scales were hard like cement. They took the place of sidewalks all over town. All across the country. And all those years while we were walking on them, they were listening and watching. Learning all about us humans. And we might never ever know."

How long would the aliens wait to attack? I wondered.

"Let's go home," said Carlos.

But I had to know more. "When would you attack?" I asked.

"Tonight," said Ethan. "No one would be expecting that. Would they?"

Caleb looked at him in surprise.

"You guys are creeping me out," said Carlos.

I looked at the sidewalk. I tried feeling it through my shoes. Was it warmer than normal? Sidewalks stayed warm after it got dark, because they held all that heat from the sun. But was that really the reason, or were they actually alive? I stared at the sidewalk in the dark. I tried to tell if it was moving. If it was breathing.

Caleb was biting his upper lip. I knew that look. He was trying hard not to laugh. I ignored him and looked up at the night sky. There were a lot of shooting stars.

"You guys . . ." said Carlos.

The sidewalk shook, like an earthquake or something really big was happening. Something really big, but really far away, and just now reaching us.

"We're just feeling a truck go by," said Caleb.

"There aren't any trucks on the street," Ethan pointed out. There weren't any cars either. It was dark, and we were the only ones around.

"Can this be happening?" I said.

I looked at the street again. Was Caleb right? No one would suspect a sidewalk. You saw them every day. Wait! I glanced at the corner of the block.

The fire hydrant was glowing. Slowly it stretched up into the air, growing like a weird metal tree.

"That's how they did it!" said Caleb. "That's their disguise!"

Ethan stood right behind me, chuckling. "Don't be stupid," he said. "Hydrants aren't alive."

The hydrant grew taller and thicker until it was the size of a car.

Suddenly, Ethan's voice changed. "They're things," he said. "Tools."

I turned around and saw a stranger wearing Ethan's clothes. His body was heavy. His arms ended in claws. His face was green and rubbery. His eyes were just slits, like a cat's.

"What do you see every day?" he said, in a thick, rubbery voice. "Your friends," he went on. "Your neighbors. But do you really know who they are? What they are?"

The stranger came closer, and the three of us, Caleb, Carlos, and I, backed up farther and farther.

Something metal clanged. Bars fell in front of us like a jail cell. We were locked inside the hydrant. It had become a sturdy steel cage.

That's when we heard the sirens go off.

And when we knew the aliens were here.

THE VOICE IN THE BOYS' ROOM

Logan needed a break from after-school band practice. He needed to use the boys' room. But he hated using it when other boys were in there. Logan needed his privacy. Which is why, during the break, he ran down the hallways and found a quiet bathroom far away from the band room.

Ah, nice. The cool, dim room was peaceful. Peaceful as a graveyard, his grandma would say.

It was soothing to his ears after the noisy music practice. A loud note — *fortissimo!* — blasted from the trombone was still pinging through his brain.

He could still hear it, standing in the boys' room. No, it was something else.

A strange voice. Talking on a cell phone, from one of the stalls.

Great. Someone was in there at the same time! Logan would have to wait until that person left before he could finish his business. He coughed. Then he cleared his throat. Hoping the person heard him and got the message: Hurry up and leave!

But no, the voice kept mumbling and mumbling.

The room was dim. There were no windows. One lightbulb in a wire cage hung from the ceiling. Slowly, Logan bent down and twisted his head to peek under the stalls. He moved carefully. He didn't want to lose his balance so that he'd have to touch the cold cement floor with his bare hands. Gross.

Logan counted the bottoms of three white toilets. No feet.

The kid must be sitting, or standing, on the toilet, talking on the phone, Logan thought.

He stood up and shook his head. He knew practically everyone in the school, but he didn't recognize the voice. The voice was deep, but it wasn't a man's voice. It definitely belonged to a kid. An older kid.

Logan recognized a few words. It wasn't as if he was trying to hear on purpose. He couldn't help it.

. . . mumble . . . underground . . . things . . . mumble . . . grave . . . mumble . . .

Afraid to make a sound, Logan stood completely still.

. . . mumble . . . water . . . mumble . . . water . . . mumble . . . everywhere . . .

He carefully tiptoed out of the boys' room and into the hall. Then he leaned against the wall and let out his breath. Who *was* that? What was he talking about? And would he ever leave the room?

Logan started hopping up and down. This was getting serious. A normal person would have finished their business by now and come out.

He crossed his legs and waited ten more minutes. He knew he should head back to the music room, but he had to go. It was building up inside him like a clogged drain. He was probably already late for the second half of practice anyway.

"Are you kidding me?" Logan cried, throwing up his arms. That was it. He was tired of waiting. Kid or no kid, he was going to use that bathroom. He walked back in. He cleared his throat and fake-sneezed so the speaker would hear him. Logan stood still. The voice had stopped.

He glanced down the row of stalls. The doors were swinging open. But he thought the middle door had been shut before.

As Logan walked past the stalls, he realized no one was there. The doors hung open and no one was sitting inside.

Had the voice come from a vent somewhere? Could it have been someone out in the hall, echoing off the dirty wall tiles?

Logan did what he came to do. Then he stood at the sink and washed his hands.

He heard the voice behind him.

. . . mumble . . . underneath . . . mumble . . . water . . . inside . . .

It was coming from the middle stall. Logan shuffled over to the half-open door. He could see the toilet, the silver pipes, the pile of paper towels, and the stupid graffiti on the walls. Another mumble came from the toilet itself. Logan took a few more steps.

A cell phone floated in the water.

Okay. Some kid had dropped his phone without realizing it, and his friend was still talking on the other end. Weird. It looked like a nice phone. The owner would want it back. *I'll take it to the lost and found,* thought Logan.

Then he thought, *Why me?*

Then he thought, *Okay, it's only water.* Logan stooped down to pick up the lost, mumbling phone.

A hairless hand reached up from inside the toilet and grabbed him.

It started to pull.

ABOUT THE AUTHOR

Michael Dahl, the author of the Library of Doom and Troll Hunters series, is an expert on fear. He is afraid of heights (but he still flies). He is afraid of small, enclosed spaces (but his house is crammed with over 3,000 books). He is afraid of ghosts (but that same house is haunted). He hopes that by writing about fear, he will eventually be able to overcome his own. So far it is not working. But he is afraid to stop. He claims that, if he had to, he would travel to Mount Doom in order to toss in a dangerous piece of jewelry. Even though he is afraid of volcanoes. And jewelry.

ABOUT THE ILLUSTRATOR

Xavier Bonet is an illustrator and comic-book artist who resides in Barcelona. Experienced in 2D illustration, he has worked as an animator and a background artist for several different production companies. He aims to create works full of color, texture, and sensation, using both traditional and digital tools. His work in children's literature is inspired by magic and fantasy as well as his passion for the art.

MICHAEL DAHL TELLS ALL

Do you know how a pearl is formed? A tiny grain of sand or grit gets trapped inside the slippery gut of an oyster. Juices from the oyster stick to the grain and harden, covering it layer by layer. The bit of sand grows into a beautiful shiny glob — a pearl. That's how stories are formed, too. Some tiny idea or inspiration, like a birthday party or a cuckoo clock or a noise in an empty bathroom, gets stuck in my brain. More ideas come along and get stuck to the first idea, building it up layer by layer, sentence by sentence. And the result? A nice spooky glob called a story. Here's where some of the stories in this book began.

DON'T MAKE A WISH

There's an **old saying:** Be careful what you wish for, because it might come true. How bad could a wish be, especially at a fun event like a birthday party? I like to use this formula for scary stories: start with something happy or cheerful, and then see what could possibly go wrong.

HAIKUKU

Making up **haiku**, a form of Japanese poetry, has been a pastime of mine since I learned what they were in fourth grade. Recently I read a scary haiku by the author Katherine Applegate, creator of Animorphs and *The One and Only Ivan.* She inspired me to make my own spooky mini-tale, in only seventeen syllables.

BLINK!

One of my favorite **Doctor Who** episodes is called "Blink." It's about evil statues that move toward you when you're not looking! I challenged myself to think up a story that would be completely different but would have the same name. Blinking made me think of eyes, and that made me think of eye doctors, and that made me think of eye drops. And drops made me think of elevators. Weird, I know. But that's where stories come from.

SNOW MONSTER

One of my favorite kinds of stories is where you're reading along, minding your own business, and then someone drops a **plot twist** and — boom! — everything changes. Then you go back and reread the story to find out how you were tricked. Once you know the trick, you can't wait to re-watch the film or reread the book and see how it all fits together. I used the snowy woods as a backdrop because of hunting stories I've heard from friends in Minnesota, Wisconsin, and Iowa.

A PERFECT FIT

Sleepovers are the perfect time for telling scary stories. What if having a sleepover was the scary story? The story's subject came from my memories of middle and high school. I always disliked cliques, those special little groups where all the members look and act and sound alike. Are they robots, or worse . . . ?

SIDEWALKS FROM OUTER SPACE

When I was in fourth and fifth grade, I had a recurring **nightmare about aliens** landing in my backyard. My friends and I tried to hide behind trees and bushes, but we were always caught. That's when I woke up, breathing hard and staring out the window to make sure I didn't see fleets of ships hanging in the night sky. I think I was freaked out after watching the 1953 sci-fi movie *Invaders from Mars* on TV. (Here's a weird note: the film's writer was inspired by a dream his wife had about aliens invading the planet. Hmm. What do you call it when different people have the same dream? Creepy!)

THE VOICE IN THE BOYS' ROOM

Quiet, **empty restrooms** (for boys or girls) are just plain spooky. Period. This story gives one reason why!

GLOSSARY

alien (AY-lee-uhn) — a being from another planet

bloodthirsty (BLUHD-thur-stee) — taking pleasure in violence

destruction (di-STRUHK-shuhn) — something that has been destroyed

disguised (dis-GIZED) — hid something, usually having to do with your appearance

earthquake (URTH-kwayk) — a sudden, violent shaking of the earth, which may damage buildings

gossip (GAH-sip) — to talk about other people's personal business

graffiti (gruh-FEE-tee) — art or words people put on walls and other surfaces where they're not supposed to be

infection (in-FEK-shuhn) — an illness caused by bacteria or a virus

introduced (in-truh-DOOST) — made to be known to others by name

invasion (in-VAY-zhuhn) — attack made on a country or other place

jealous (JEL-uhss) — feeling resentful of someone because they have something you want

mumble (MUHM-buhl) — to speak quietly and unclearly

privacy (PRYE-vuh-see) — when a person is not seen or disturbed by anyone else

sirens (SYE-ruhns) — devices that make a loud, shrill noise

stealth (STELTH) — a secret, clever way of behaving

suspect (suh-SPEKT) — to think something may be true

DISCUSSION QUESTIONS

1. In "Sidewalks from Outer Space," a group of boys encounters an alien on their walk home from the movie theater. What do you think happens after the story ends? Discuss what the alien invasion might look like.

2. Logan hears a voice in the story "The Voice in the Boys' Room," and he thinks there is another kid in the bathroom at the same time as him. Soon he realizes that there's no one there, but the voice continues. If you were in Logan's position, would you have left the bathroom earlier? Talk about why or why not.

3. In "Don't Make A Wish," what do you think the wish was that Nina made?

WRITING PROMPTS

1. In the story "A Perfect Fit," Lola is having trouble fitting in at her new school. Have you ever had trouble fitting in? Write a paragraph about it.

2. In "Snow Monster," a father and son are out hunting when they come across signs that the Geeshee Moogomon has been near by. Imagine you are the monster, and write the story from your point of view.

3. "Haikuku" follows a form of poetry called the haiku. A haiku has three lines. The first line is five syllables, the second is seven syllables, and the third is five syllables. Write a spooky haiku of your own!

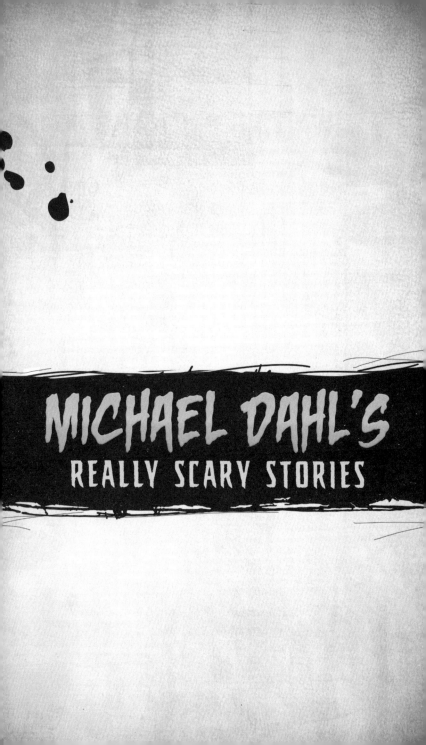

MICHAEL DAHL'S
REALLY SCARY STORIES